RED SUGAR, NO MORE.

Red Sugar, No More

RED SUGAR, NO MORE.

SIJDAH HUSSAIN

One Step at a Time

Word by Word

Sijdah Hussain is a debut, modern-day, *Messy* writer who works as a Content Marketer in Lahore, Pakistan. While her writing is mostly based on experiences and other real-life inspirations, it does have a flavour of hyperbole at some points. She first got the idea to turn her poems cum songs into a chapbook when she started to see a pattern in them. They were all intricately intertwined to form something more than just one song or two. This is a story of someone going through a rush of emotions from blaming others to herself, every now and then.

Sijdah is currently writing her second book of the Sugar series, hoping the best for this one. She plans to publish a book series with a variety of styles to tell a coming of age story starting from hatred and moving towards self-actualization. It revolves around a 21-year-old who finds out life just isn't what she thought it to be. She's still finding words to blurt out her feelings in this part.

Just know that you are not alone in this world even when you feel like it's the end. She's here to help you be your saviour just as she was her own because at the end – no one else can do it for you!
You can connect to her via Instagram (@sijdah).

www.thesugarseries.com

Red Sugar, No More

ISBN 979-8-6400-4064-7

www.thesugarseries.com

Acknowledgements

Every single tear that trickles down your cheek - leaves you in the middle of a two-way road. It is on you, how you conjure up the courage, to choose which path you want to continue on for the rest of the journey. I, too, have had the opportunity to choose not just once but many a time and I am thankful to every single soul from my cats to the humans who made me choose light even after drifting into the dark. If you say or believe you haven't or wouldn't stand at such a place - you're lucky and ignorant to nature's way of helping us grow. This pain is a necessary element for you and I. Therefore, just accept it and rise from the muddy waters like a pretty lotus flower.

I'd like to take this opportunity to thank my family for the immense support throughout my life and the phases of depression it offered – without questions. I'd also like to thank the professor who failed me, **Umer Khan**, for making sure that I only passed my courses if I understood poetry but most of all I'd like to express my gratitude for **Saima Jabeen** for helping me through my rough time and making sure I complete my thesis. **Nida Shah** - I love you for your mere existence - I feel our souls are truly old friends.

To my parents, **Muhammad Saleem Abbas** & **Nuzhat Rana** *(yeah, my mom kept here surname)* thank you for making me believe in myself every time I didn't want to. More importantly, thank you so much for giving me the opportunity to be born out of love, warmth and so much more.

To my sister, **Wajdaan Muhammad**, thank you for tolerating me at my worst and playing the elder sister despite being younger when I am at my breaking point (every time).

To my present friends and those from my past/future - que sera, sera - whether we stay in touch or not I am here for you all. Whether I was/am/get angry about something just know that none of you is or ever will be replaced by the other - you all hold a special place in my heart even if you broke it intentionally or unintentionally.

You all played a vital role in making me the woman I am today and I am nothing but proud of my growth. Thus, thank you!

www.thesugarseries.com

Trigger Warning:

This book contains a rush
of emotions - sometimes
rolling in the same rink
over and over & other
times hopping from one
rollercoaster to another.

Be sure to be merciful to
your mental health
throughout this journey
and after. You are
amazing.

Only you can save
yourself and maybe pets ...
yes, cats, dogs etc. can
help you , plants too!

Introduction

We all have our moments of glory and obscurity, this chapbook touches down on every feeling a human being comes across. This book, in general, is an outcome of one's intense desire to be validated and needed. We tend to find ***Horcruxes in humans***. A different concept - who'd have thought it like that, right? I know I didn't back in time when I derived happiness, strength and calamity from humanistic bonds. Imagining future trips, being our own people, pulling each other up – until a dry spell took hold of it all.

Depression, a lot like the **Great Depression** of '20s-'30s, has people swirling for quite a time in their own created labyrinths. Mine didn't begin with a stock market crash, *haha*, it began with failure in love – I guess. And, now that I think over it – maybe that is how it begins for all of us. Distances over significant others and their pathetic-ity, protecting the peers who probably wouldn't give two craps about us, hiding things out of love to protect each other. It's absurd, how everyone eyed our pack from the beginning – saying it was bound to have a crack so big we just wouldn't know what hit us. Many forces tried – but until we trusted and made each other the priority … no one ever succeeded.

You know as per psychology, a break up supposedly takes only 6 months of healing to move on. The pain reduces significantly and one is able to see positivity around him/her. I couldn't for a whole year – not because my Horcruxes were won over by someone else but because they chose to be with that someone else over me. I wasn't the priority anymore. Missed tests, deadlines, assignments – got late, stopped brushing hair and teeth … didn't even get out of bed for days. Not a single ping on my mobile to ask if I were okay.

"Maybe they were already too tired and this was what was needed for so long. This falling out was bound to happen with or without the Lucifer involved."

I got a book, read the same lines over and over, in desperation to just pass the time and get out of those tall towers which (for quite a long time) I called home. Everyone gave me a new reason to never believe in another human ever again. This book inculcates all those feelings, hurt, understandings and acceptance to move forward. **Taylor Swift**, a singer, and **Nashville**, a TV show, inspired me to write my heart out lyric by lyric and I did. Each song within this book is an outcome of my heart's melodious outburst. The words are messy and raw just like my thoughts at the time. Thus, **Dear Reader**, this is just a beginning of our journey together - we will mount those horses once again and rise to our full potential with each passing book, each passing page – poem – monologue and much more with each passing dawn.

More power to our bond and us!

Red Sugar (also known as brown sugar) comes from sugar cane and is the purest form of sweetness one can get their hands on. It is good for health due to the antioxidants present within it.

<u>Accounted Messes</u>

I need to keep going.
I am happy, ~~now~~ sometimes.

~~I will get through this.~~

~~Maybe it's for the best!~~

I can't! I need to keep going.
I can't!
I can't! I can't!
I can't!
I can't! I can't!
I can't!
I can't! I can't! I will ~~not~~. I need to keep going.
I can't! I can't!
I can't! I need to keep going.
I can't! I can't! I need to keep going.
I can't! I can't!
I can't! I can't!
I can't! I can't! I need to keep going.
I can't! I need to keep going.
I can't! I need to keep going.
I can't! I can't! I ~~cannot~~.
I can't! I can't!
I need to keep going.
I need to keep going.

This is a story of:

light & dark moon & stars hurt & heart

A human   A Woman

A bird   A man   A key

A friendship A relationship A sinking ship

Anger   Hope   Grief
Dismay   A cat   A plant

A knight   A dog stray

love & hate

A cage   A knife

And endless preys

Succumbed together
Suppressed b e l o w
t h e layers ofs k i n
& b l o o d vessels
t u r n e d **black**
't i s a story
of a heart
burnt to
r o t
!

 Red Sugar, No More

In this part

there's no you & I

just an emptiness

filling my mind

with screams

and cries

icecream

dipped

fries.

This is the

part where

it all begins

the journey

to not the

centre of

earth

but

me!

This is the part of anguish grey

curtains blue & wallpapers yellow

t h i s is the p a r t where I learn

to lose you & try to gain me back

this is a part where the end is

my s t a r t !

Red Sugar, No More

18

Sometimes –

you & I just don't exist

and that's alright!

20

<u>You & Me</u>

(To the ones I lost and left)

4/14/2017

You & Me,

Baby, we were never meant to be!

You like living in an illusion while for me life itself is quite a fusion.

You like to make everyone feel important while I tend to keep all at a certain distance.

The reason, however, is the same for us both - no matter how different we might be.

We are just scared little infants who can't afford a broken heart.

So you just tend to run while I stand stern.

You twist your words & I twist my feelings.

A twist is inevitable but un-assured for what or when or when & where...

You & Me – we just never were meant to be.

In distress, you like hiding while I act as a wild-ing.

Now that it's the end, let's smile because as little as it might be – we were good, it was good, we did good.

If **ever** it's me who you miss

Just smile because now I'll be away a zillion miles … and sorry but no kiss.

Let us now wipe away the foggy memories from our mirror of life

'Cuz baby you & me –

We were never meant to be.

It's just, my dear, you & I

We're nothing more than a sigh.

Confusion is a stairway to clarity, in a way.

Sometimes, we cross it quickly & other times we make it our home.

It just takes a little patience & retracing of steps to be back on the way.

<u>Deadliest Affair(s)</u>

5/10/2017

Deadliest affair with a fierce blare
Ferocious the better
Catering like a waiter
Holding it more tightly
So we could go a bit slightly
Do you know what's mightier?

Growing up to be weirder!
Because it's already there & you don't need no despair.
So let's just clear this stagnant air

Let's stow away all fears
'Cuz now we're in our tears;
Crying away all fears

Oh dear, oh dear
Oh dear, oh dear

Don't let it wear
Just clear and steer
Devastated in a second so mere

Boiling in my care
Such in shear, such in shear
So let's just bear
And … dare to care?

Don't come near
Until we know, we stand where!
And all is fair & clear

You're just a part of my tear

Which was dear is no longer beloved

As all the changed paths were enforced

Until we were forced to put on a course

Jotted down so now you calm down

It takes me, it takes me
Wonder why it just kills me.

Haha and *bills* me for all those delicate thrills
Drills me _{just drills me} until there is no will
Dedicated moans of all those *bears* and ^{lions}
Kills me for all that you are galore
Just to lead me so I further explore

Me and my pain
You & your vain.

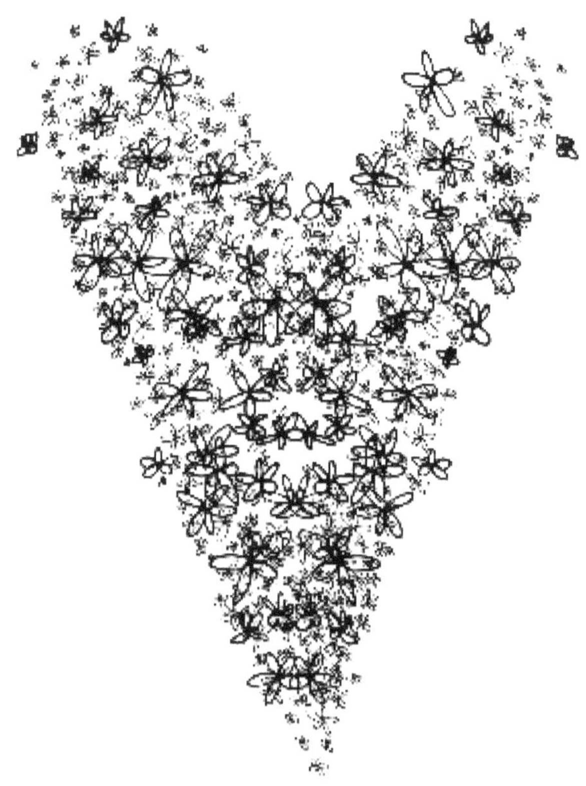

*In the earliest English, the word **bully** was created by borrowing **boel** from the Dutch language. It means lover or sweetheart. Today, it is used to talk about someone who gets off by intimidating others because making others feel inferior is the only way for them to feel better about themselves maybe.*

Oh, how the words have fallen – literally fallen from grace!

<u>My Social Bully</u>

7/11/2017

I know a girl who's a social bully

She's not yet aware of it … fully

But whenever she wants

She hurts and taunts

Highlighting her talents — *she usually just flaunts*

I know a girl who's a social bully

She wraps you around her fingers … fully

She'd slit your trust --

and crap you with her secretive unruly

Giving out and about;

saying she understands you totally!

But you, you, you are just too naïve

to understand my point

Don't publicize your social joint --

She says you're running after a tag by this

When in reality, it was her wish!

Her wish to be publically known

Even if it was from something … she had stolen

I know a girl who's a social bully

You could never know who she is truly

Blinded by platonic love

You let her put you on a stove

I know a girl who's a social bully

She smiles and enchants

Only for her boasts – to win the last word
And when you disagree
With her **undying purity** – cruel she will be

Ripping you
Dipping you
In a lifelong guilt
Not for disagreeing but for offering her your quilt

The best way to avoid
Is truly to just be devoid
Pain is important
It is in your fate
To help you stand straight
For when the next social climber knocks at your gate
Remember this & don't end up being a bait --
Learn for it's never too late

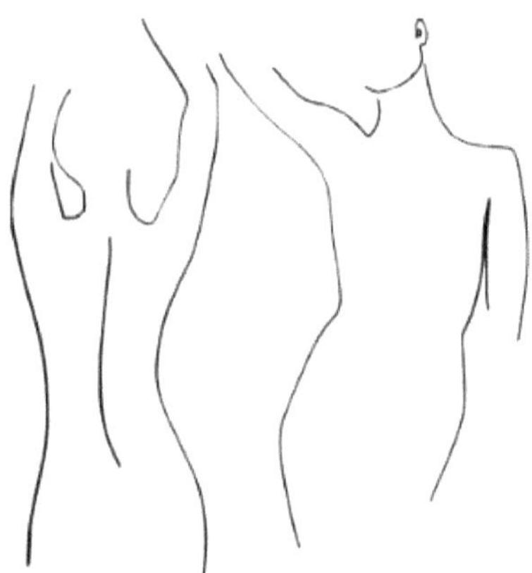

Like the roots stay forever with trees, help them grow and make them strong,
will you stay with me just a bit long(er)?

<u>Stay</u>

7/20/2017

You want to stay
But you can't say

There's just so much fear on its way
Consuming our hopes from the
last radiant ray leaving us
completely astray

We all have our demons to fight
So let's take this beautiful long slide
Even if it is from a great height
Just know that this is our right
Come on and enjoy this ride
As our smiles go wide
With each tide

Stow away the worries
Stow away the queries
Eat the blackberries
Even if we are not a
lasting *friends' series*

Let's just have each other to patronize

For we're no more wise
But surely it won't suffice
To hold unto disguise

It's okay to care
As long as we're here
Let's not go elsewhere
'Cuz in my heart it's very fair
Oh no, don't shed a tear
'Cuz we're in the clear

Red Sugar, No More

So let's just hold hands, my dear
It's time for us to just be here

It's time for us to just be here
Just. Here.

Hey Gurllll!

Introduce me to that bird?

Can I have that plant's number?

Could you do my music assignment?

Here, hold my beanie.

Gotta go, byeee!

<u>Door Mat</u>

9/8/2017

The door to the mat or mat to the door
It didn't really make a difference –
as I was just set to ***bore***!
So many, oh my dear
I just had to bear
'Cuz they didn't have with them
A well enough gear
Peeling off my layers
Readying for all the affairs
Oh, I am rubbed!

RUBBED

AND

RUGGED

<u>as I stay</u>
On my fate, I dismay
On this cold floor as I just lay

I remember …
Each day
I remember …
Each way

And all they ever had to do was say —

With all the feet as they would crush
Little gentle strokes with their
sharp & bejewelled brush!
Sharp – but bejewelled – brush.

No matter if it was a spill or a gush
I never really did ever just hush
Anyone;
Anyone.

Picked me up and played around

Making me think I am a worthy crown

When all I really was … just brown

Pretty lipsticks and expensive gowns

All went through ~~me~~ —
Since
    I
      was
        the
          only
            passageway
               to glory town!

                    Nervous laughs and crooked smiles

As they exchanged secret piles

                    Moving along, taking a dive

Planning to only run over me alive

I was the whore
I was bound to bore

    It didn't matter whether it was door to the mat or mat to the door
    Then came the time to throw me out as I got gore
And just like an unwanted crack in the floor
      I was out the door
Waiting it out until someone else
Picked me up to place me by their

      DOOR!

             Oh yes, another door —
             This might be a story
             Of partnered glory

But oh my, my,
How have I forgotten?
It did not freaking matter …
    whether it was a mat to the door or a door to the mat
Then three cats comfortably on me sat
    Reminding me it's better to bear their fat —
      Then being a plain ol' door mat!

    A. PLAIN. OLD. DOOR. MAT.

Healing is Messy!

Life isn't in our brain // It flows through our veins.

Just a little cut to drain out the galaxies that keep me up tonight.

Just a little cut and all this goes away. Just a little cut and no more thoughts.

No memories. No pain. I mean screw nostalgia. I don't want it. Take it back!

<u>The End</u>

10/11/2017

Do you ever feel like
> it's the end of your time?
> Wanting your body

to give in to every pine
> > Acting outside as if everything is fine
> > When in reality you break a little
> > more with every chime?

^{Decaying} and _{rotting} with each new <u>face</u>

Twisting a knife in your ^{back} *resting their case*

Headaches, _{heartbreaks} come running to your door

As you just sit there staring at the cold *dark* f l o o r?

> Those **warm** memories, those words of **promises**

Suffocate every <u>inch</u> of you forming a pRiSoN
> Sinking in deep, taking you to the verge – just jump

To stop you from trying to break free —

<u>It just can't let you be!</u>

You have to accept the reality
> > Humans are just as they can be

Morals or sins, it doesn't make much difference today
> > For you, dear love, would always be the MAYDAY

The pounding in your head
> > > The squishing of your heart

> Old friends will turn and create excuses to part

Sometimes, it'd be for their love,

Sometimes their egos

Whatever, ^{whoever}, would drive you away …

would laugh from behind those windows grey.

Go steady and behold,

Friendships these days are easily ^{bought} and _{sold}

Takes no time to turn warm hearts cold

Taking away your sweetness

Only to leave you when

YOU are no longer the golden fruit

It is life; life is it?

People can be cruel and so be it

You will decay, yes, you will!

There's not much to change but try as you can still.

Stop with those cuts

Stop with those 'buts'

Don't try to force

your eyelids shut

Keep going, my soul

Keep going, my heart

They can't decide your fate

Those cheap old tarts!

Another stranger, another dream.
& my unending silent screams ~

Red Sugar, No More

10/2/2017

There's something

Something that's back!

Under the bed or waiting near the rack

As I lay and try not to quack

I shut my eyes tighter

Taking His name

Believing that this time at least – He'd have it tamed

Remembering and reciting verses hard in sleep —

But all in vain

Just … all in vain.

Vain and pain struggle together

Making me open my eyes, as I stay frozen

Frozen for minutes, seconds or hours —

I know not

For the heart just tries to be a bit brazen.

I hear noises wherever I go

They just play with my head no matter how much I stow

There are no heroes --

No scouts or even floors but only crows

There are no shows

-- no one to hear out your silent shouts

I hear waves

I hear breaths

As I lose my mind to tiny shreds

The heart skips its beat

As there's crawling on my sheets

Red Sugar, No More

Then I feel a tingle on my feet --
Thinking the feet are only going numb
I start to hear a familiar hum
Breathing progresses near my ear
As I try to steer my mind clear
I stop breathing —
It never does
As I feel a constant buzz

It creeps unto me
Slowly pressing --
Pulling my hair
Feeling my skin
Not sure, however, if it's a witch or djin

And then it shakes me inside out
Making me pant when I can't even shout!
Ask my heart and ask my guts
We know there's something that needs to be shut
Me or it?
Not too sure
Oh, but I can't take this anymore!

This leads me to think, picturing every time
Someone there to save me from this crime
Just having someone to guard me on times like these —
To … be my keys

After taking the time to normalize
I think '*what to do*' – so the moment is never revised
But there's nothing …
They say it's nothing

Red Sugar, No More

Come on, it's nothing more than a sleep paralysis
But, oh all those nail pierces and horror kisses —
Forcing one to make death wishes!?

So let's hope I die
Before its next try!
For I don't want needles or a grope
The next time I sleep or so I hope!

Now every time I'll just go and have my coffee —
As it is the only way that's going to keep me from being its t o f f e e.

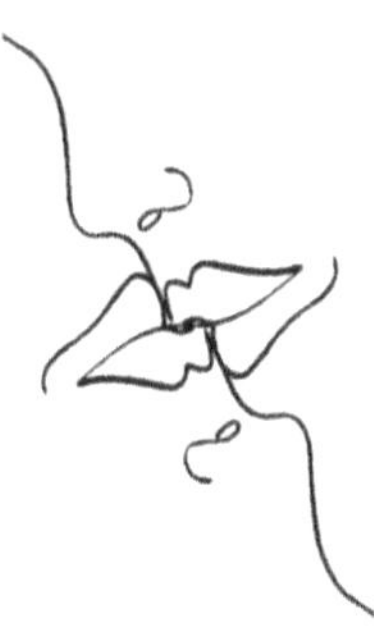

I LOAF YOU

Life isn't just about getting lemons out of it. An unexpected turn and a kind smile warms you up on the coldest of days.

Something

11/5/2018

There is something

Something about you –

Like the dust of stars

The pain in wars

The light of a dim room

The moon between all the shiny stars

There is something

Something inside you

The boldness of a mountain

The laughter from the hollows

Darkness in an alley

Depth of a valley

Truth and honesty

Yet filled with a righteous brutality

The shine in your eyes

Oh, the way you smile!

Making others want to go all the extra miles

Pushing them to be worthwhile

From their own selves and not just for you

There is something

You're the bright in night

The moon to my stars

I'll chase you forever

Even with all the scars – yours & mine!

For there is something,

Something … about you!

Shared gender or shared hearts

I know you would help me

pull out from my back that frozen <u>shards</u> ~

Something … about you.

55

You can get addicted to a living being too,
a beautiful feeling – dangerous but beautiful.

<u>Wired</u>

12/7/2017

There's a company
Filled with a different symphony

The smile

The joys

Being each other's favourite toys

The sun ^{turns} dark

The night _{owls} bark

Sitting under the skies   in a well-lit park

Mountains climb up the treeS

The world takes a shift –
We're in a parallel universe

There's no curse

No money, no money in my purse

Life is like *The Book's* beautiful ^{verse}.

Bounties, Wealth and Pleasure

Finding in each other so much leisure

Seeking each other like a holy treasure

Before we get to have a proper burial

Rising up from our hollow graves

Self-inflicted pains all gone

Stitching back together

what was once torn

Pulling out that once was locked away

Being … for what we used to cry & pray

Never letting us astray
Creating our own happy days

In the **hazy mist** of shambles

Coming out of all the pain that ^{crumbles}

Inside, *twist and hammers*, the inside

Being the smiles spread across wide

With each passing tide

As with the rules, we abide

Never getting tired.

To you; I'm totally wired!

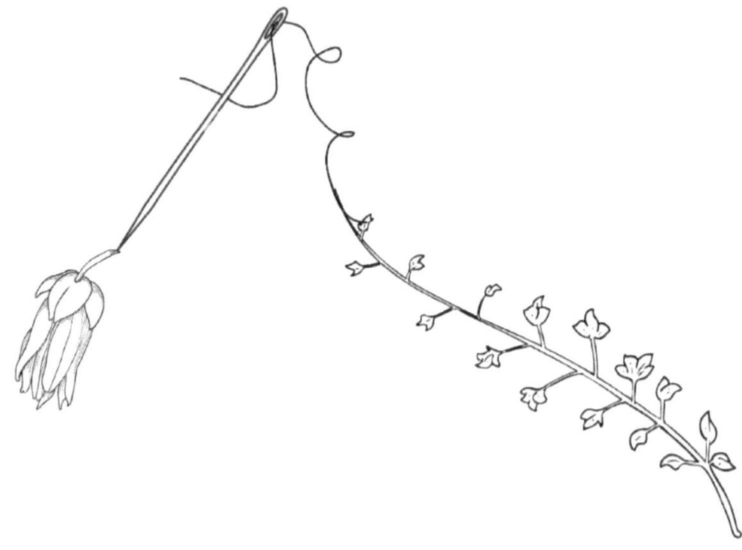

*Disappointments and humanity go hand in hand & there's absolutely nothing
we can do about it – other than taking the first step by setting an example
ourselves but remember even Superman was hated by
Lex Luthor (a "friend" at first; a foe later).*

<u>Soil the Loyals</u>

12/8/2017

The hollow darkness
Always follows sharpness
Betting at loyals
Bringing upon inner toils
Burning out the friendship foils
Leaving us hanging as the blood boils
As the blood boils.

Leaves turn brown
Crunching all o'er the ground
Making us hell-bound
As we seek comfort by not being around –
Those who were the reason for our wound

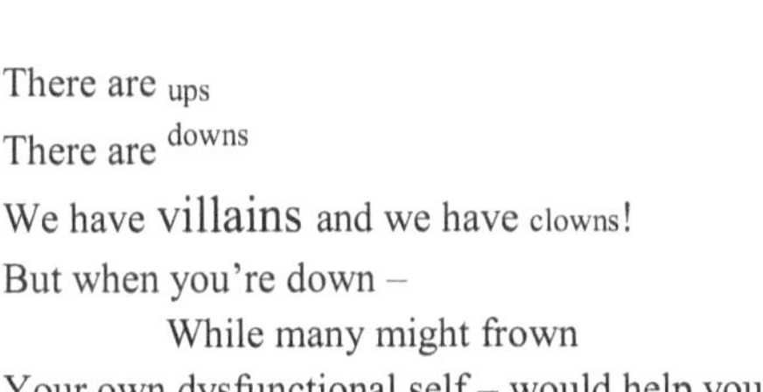

Sadness enveloping
the outside sun
Life being too much of a pun
Dragging to the head a metal gun
Ourselves, ourselves –
we need to shun!?

There are ups
There are downs
We have villains and we have clowns!
But when you're down –
While many might frown
Your own dysfunctional self – would help you
get back your golden gown

For when you are with yourself,
nothing can pull you down
Yourself, just trust.
Breathe

You're your loyal, set yourself free!

RIP
humanity

*The saddest thing you can do as a human is to discuss one person with another for the sake of it. The unkindest thing you can do to a human is to tarnish their reputation in front of others just to make yourself look good. An unfortunate thing that you can do to a person is to be unapologetically direct and not understand their side. However, the WORST thing **you** can do is to slip in **'little'** white lies just to save yourself from confrontations & emotional conversations.*

*Complain about each other to **each other.***

Have your freedom ... G E N T L Y.

Discuss your mind – politely.

<u>Lies in Disguise</u>

12/22/2017

Lies, lies

All around like flies

Escaping the mouths of not friends but spies

All the *'hi(s)'* and *'goodbyes'*

Just turning to dark no matter how radiant the light

As we take a dangerous flight

       Called Life.

Called Life!

           No, love, no one would ever stay by your side

           Lie and lies,

           To bleed your eyes

           'Cuz well, oh bitch, surprise!!

           This world can't be rid of the vice

Circling around

Pulling one under the ground

Every inch they'd like to pound

Breaking other's crowns

Headaches and frowns

Preying on everyone in the happy towns

Using other's skins to make their own golden gowns

           Bashing, ranting and a killing spree

           Gaslighting others not knowing they're done so

           by the same fire-lovers

       Asses so full of shit it's ogling out their mouths

Red Sugar, No More

No baby, no one is nice for free

You need to be a large oak tree

Bearing benefits for others to take and

just be!

Until you get too weak and almost die

Oh no, no, they won't leave you alone

They'd bring the axe to chop you down

To make a fire & set it to your,

yes, your gown!

Go baby go – go lie on the ground
Don't make that face – you look as if you're dumbfounded!

You, baby, you were born for every single wound

Even when you'd lay in your **tomb**

People would always spit and pee

On your grave and that too for <u>free</u>!

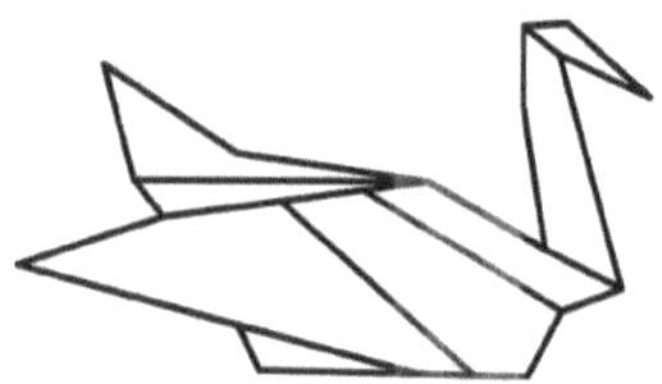

*It only takes a few words, a little distance & a whole lot of suppressed emotions
to move out of the primary label and press delete on each other.*

<u>Beast Friends</u>

3/22/2018

From where I look, it's always been this way
You talk,

        we talk

           and

             just talk

               And talk about nothing to do with what's necessary or not

        You

        go & go ~

        just go like the wind

      Leaving my world too humid to comfortably live in!

And we wander ~

      just wander into oblivion

        Looking for a *Safe Haven*

          What we forgot was that until **we** wander or stay or play

        Together, together & together
We'll never ever be any better

      'Cuz, my dear,
    we're the monsters living under each other's bed
     Dwelling within each other's head.

Sweethearts, all your pretty stars
Gave me quite some scars

         You might have gone a little too far
      But you aren't going to be my death -- my tar
    You were my downfall --
You were my favourite bar

        AND

While; I'll be a galaxy
You'd always be just stars

     My little, little scars
     My little glitter stars

       Meet every day, drive cool cars
      But oh - little twinkle stars …

Red Sugar, No More

I have my own powers

I'll find my way back to the towers

Oh, my dear, little bitter stars

Note that I won't spew venom

as you all did even from afar

And still, I'll win the war

Because it's not you whom

I need to win from

It is from the feelings

You left behind when I was torn

I will rise again

Like a phoenix from the ashes

Be my own person again

Handing out umbrellas in heavy rain.

It's so overwhelming when you notice how the clock ticks; so many tiny pieces holding each other together just so it keeps going. We are like clocks, too! Always ticking to the tocks. When the pieces of our soul are torn away or broken – we can't be sent to the mending shop, however. So how do we get better? Workable? Thoughts can be tiring, at times. Or maybe it's the same time – who knows? The clock is broken. Meh.

72

Task

3/22/2018

I am tired, ^{tired}

Of my brain being so twisted and wired, _{wired}

Oh, how can I just get it fired, _{fired}?

Get a new one hired, ^{hired}?

Sometimes I just want to be

A beautiful *melancholic* catastrophe

But is that a trophy?

Not for one, not for two –

not for anyone, baby

It makes me tired, _{tired}

Because my brain is

overly wired, ^{wired}

The world's so quiet, quiet

Tired, _{tired}

Wash off all the stains

Given by all those in pure vain

Wash off all the bloody scars

Around them make a tattoo full of stars!

Because; ***up***

above

the world

so high – *like a diamond in the sky?*

^Why does this happen?

ʜow does this happen?

Is there a way to learn the lesson?
Is there a way to make it a weapon?

Destroy those who destroy me?

Break off their insanity

Just like they destroy me!

Oh, just like they destroy me?

Calling upon the skies
Wishing for true ties
Often do I forget --

I am just a maggot

In a world of giants made of glass

Shattering egos with each pass
Trying to be full of class

Oh let's ruin her she seems like a fun task!

'Let's bend and twist
Till her insides wish
For a death over life
As long as she's not being a hurtful wife!

Let's punch and crunch
Hate on the new girl a bunch
Until she cries
Bading the world goodbyes ...

Let's make her scream
Let's enjoy her tears like in our not-so-creepy dream

Let's grope and mope up everything good in her
Objectifying and sexualising – that's the way, baker

Put her in the oven until she's hot
and red to be served
Make her feel inferior
Wanting death – the superior!

Tired, tired

Oh so wired, wired!!

Why can't I just be?

A living catastrophe!

Tired,

tired

Tired,

tired

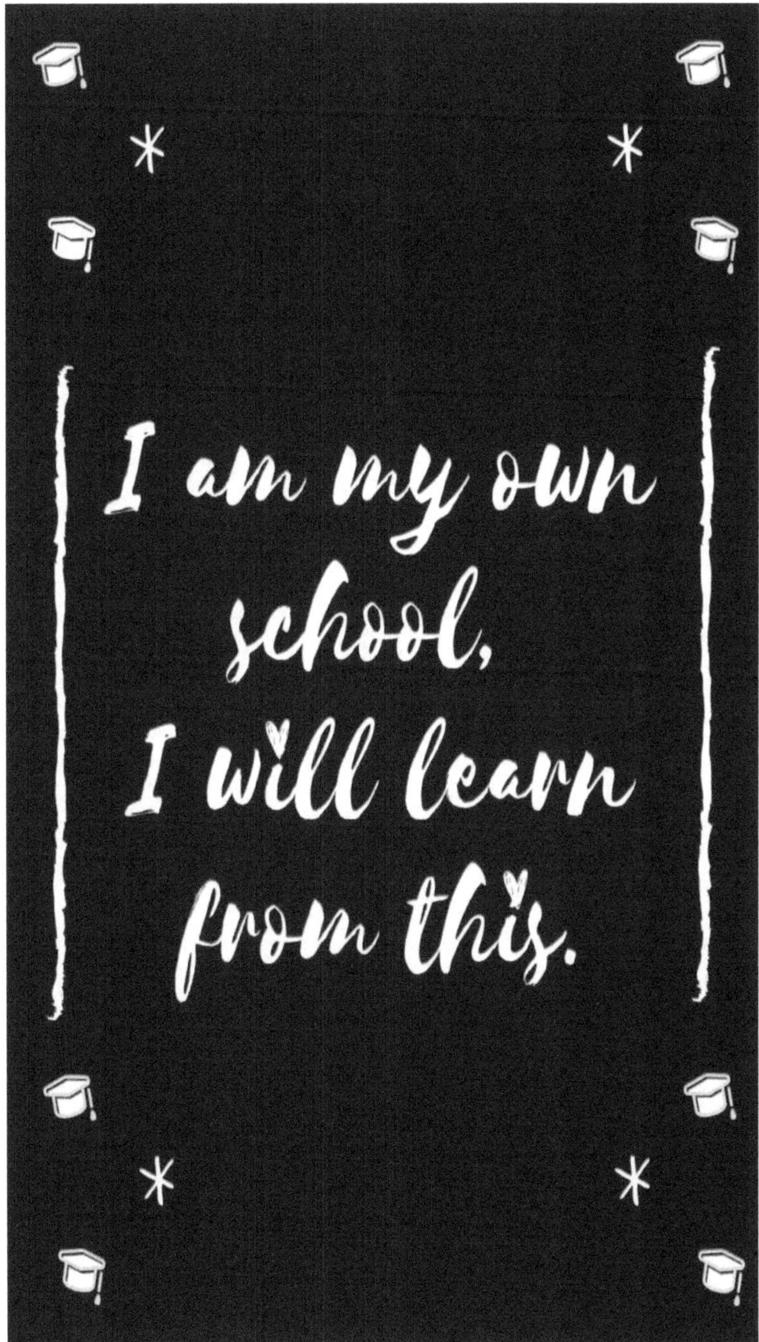
I am my own
school,
I will learn
from this.

Sometimes, no matter how hard we try for someone and hope that they will get better in time – they never do. Abusive relationships shouldn't have a key to your chambers of heart. Hold your key and keep it close. Don't end up getting addicted to such pain or human beings – for that matter. You might not be Thor but they can surely be Loki & hold you prisoner to their trickster nature.

The Pain in Trust

3/22/2018

This is the difference between ^you^ and ^I^

You ask − I give … I ask – you complain

You tell – I listen … I tell – I listen

I ^prioritize^ … you ~demoralize~

I ~kneel~ … you look ^down^

I respect … you form an ego

I give way to *love* … you end it with a *split*

        I let you win … you make me lose

        I want to trust … you just hurt too much

You are chalk and I am cheese

             You are born just to squeeze

       I am born just to excuse

You are butter and I am mere grease

           Bursting balloons with a wheeze

       Oh geez! Was that your heart?

       Is that blood oozing out of that cut?

       It's alright, things get better as time struts

       Time flew away? That's okay!

       We'd be the same, I'd always be

       your *Utgarda-Loki*

Red Sugar, No More

No one shall know, act very well

This thing between us

It's just for lust

Power, money, sex and whatnot?

I'd be your *heroine*

Here to keep you **from** *ever* leaving ~

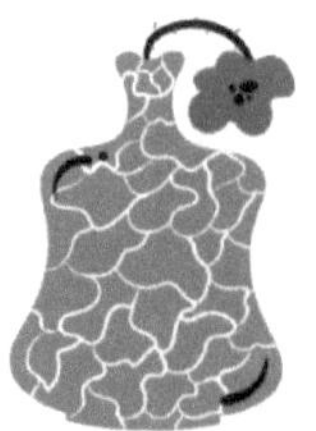

It's the memories that we yearn for & cherish – not the relationship or person when sadness engulfs our heart and makes us go through the whole storyline again and again and again and again. Those memories are not even real. They are an idea of the memory formed that day – gorgeous and heartwarming – but it wasn't always that. Was it?

<u>Versace</u>

3/25/2018

Found an old memory card

In my worn-out pink leather wallet

Had it when we were a thing

That made everyone ting!

Thought I'd find you in there

But as **expected**

As **always**

You   were   not   up   to   your   p r o m i s e

Not even in memory

Not even in dreams

Just an empty

nothingness

In my tears to follow

How could you be so shallow?

How could you leave me feeling so hollow?

I didn't delete you

I didn't hide

You made me un-see things even with my eyes opened up wide

Cried, I cried – 3 years and counting for being love-lied

How could you be?

Why'd it had to be me?

I was sincere; I was loyal

The good girl that grew up believing *Disney's* fake stories

Now listed under the title of *sluts with histories*

Thank you for making me cut and **shut**   out people, feelings & myself

Not just my skin but the people with a *'but'*

'But you're not a mess

You're a game of chess

Waiting for someone stable

To power up your ruined cable

        But let me help

       Listen and empower you

      To become your calming key

      Stow away your paranoia

            But let me make you laugh

          We'd crack jokes

          We'd be friends

            Setting ourselves as the highest

               friendship trends'

You thought they'd feast on me like a prey

'But' they all stayed!

Yes, they did

      None of them on my emotionality bid

No one wanted just an availability

As per their personal utility

The one who did

        You, yes, you

        Left me alone

       on a cold hard stone!

      In the age of glitter stars and lilac lace

    I never knew you'd be my drug, my *Versace*

I loved and failed

Oh, I got so nailed

Because you broke your promise and bailed!

Loss-hurt
Loss-adaptaion

*Healing is like making **Baumkuchen** —*
it requires a lot of time, energy and patience.

<u>Cognitive Dialect</u>

3/28/2018

There is just so much confusion

My mind's filled with intrusion

Here come the horses

There comes the storm

Oh look, a pretty little worm!

Can my mind for once have form?

Am I bad?

Or am I just sad?

Who do I ask ---

and what to really bask?

Confusions pile up over each other

As we gamble - we end up more scrambled;

Funny that you mentioned

that haven't we all just wilted.

As every whore's been quilted

And every sin's been lifted.

In a net of crimson that's tilted

– that's tilted

Every theme, oh just screams!

With a zillion deferred dreams

And every preferred scream!

Lost grief; a muddy stream

Minding all that flies
        Letting out soft muffled cries
With all those goodbyes
        Hoping for the skies
Getting ready to be kissed
        Believing all those lies
Hoping that it would all go away

                with   cries

                with cries

                with

                c

                r

                i

                e

                s

We all pretend to fly [high]

Just to colour all the skies

              Up and beyond
        Being the Galaxy's happy pawn
Not passing the day with <u>mere yawns</u>

91

*From a tiny seed to dispersed pollen grains hoping to bloom someday –
everything holds a story within it. We just need to observe a little more.*

<u>Dysfunctional Ties</u>

5/20/2018

Story, ^{story}

There's a story

Of blood and sweat,

_{Unholy} glory

Filled

with tears

Making others fret

Like coffee spillage

on an expensive

carpet

_{Story,} story

Of giants and evil

Coming out of medieval

Running through the **veins**

Causing all sorts of pains

Story, story

Of courage ^{and} passion

Some old fashioned

Stars _{and} moon

Took one

for a great

noon!

Story, story

Like chocolates _{and} candies

Bittersweet fantasies

Pushing us to keep going

Going and winning

Leaving us grinning

Tearful eyes

    Heartfelt cries

        -- shall fade

    One day it'd all be

once again a clean slate!

        Pain isn't fate

        And it surely is NOT

          your rate

Breathe and lookup

One day, everyone will be awake

The fake-ness of hypocrites will shake!

        The world shall know

          When the cat will crow

      Of the truth and lies

      At last, you will be able to cut those ties

        Ties from those cries.

*The worst thing about being underweight or overweight; too dark or too white –
in short too plain and bland in someone's perception is the fact that most people
just end up talking to you because they feel you can be a good stepping stone.
And guess what – it sucks! It sucks being the ladder to so many, helping everyone
grow and bloom, only to find yourself splayed upon the mud to be used as a path
from one person to another. Not moving an inch. Just lying there on the sticky
dirt infused ground – hoping someone would help you up – no one ever comes.
The only person who can help you crawl out is **yourself**. Get up. Try. Just try.*

You ARE Enough!

<u>Bridge</u>

5/25/2018

Every day I discover something new

Every day it changes the whole view

1, 2, 3 … they click

4, 5, 6 … they flick

Loyalties and humans aren't quite 'the' combo

They tear and cut whomever they want

and that too <u>pronto</u>!

It doesn't matter how many years together you spent

They leave you like a car with a big bad dent

You soar the wild

Weeping like a child

Putting up tents

Wherever you can

Dissociating and numbing away from reality

Remember that best friend --

and, oh, that crush?

Remember those brown eyes

filled with warmth and love?

You felt like such a

peaceful dove!

You thought she'd

help you go

above

& beyond?

Haha

but

Red Sugar, No More

_{see} she pushed you in

a muddy pond!

Together on a ^{strong} sugar rush

They both knew

Where they stood …

_{for you}

But, ^{sweetie}, you never mattered to them

Despite the long talks and heartfelt conversations

He a *Casanova* and she a *klutz*

No bro code, *'no to best friend's sisters!'* Ha Ha – My butt!!

Guys over fries and misters over sisters

While you hope they get blisters –

On those lips, they kiss each other with!

Just accept the reality

Of you being a ***bridge***

Being replaced like a

pen's cartridge

Accept it and now close the fridge.

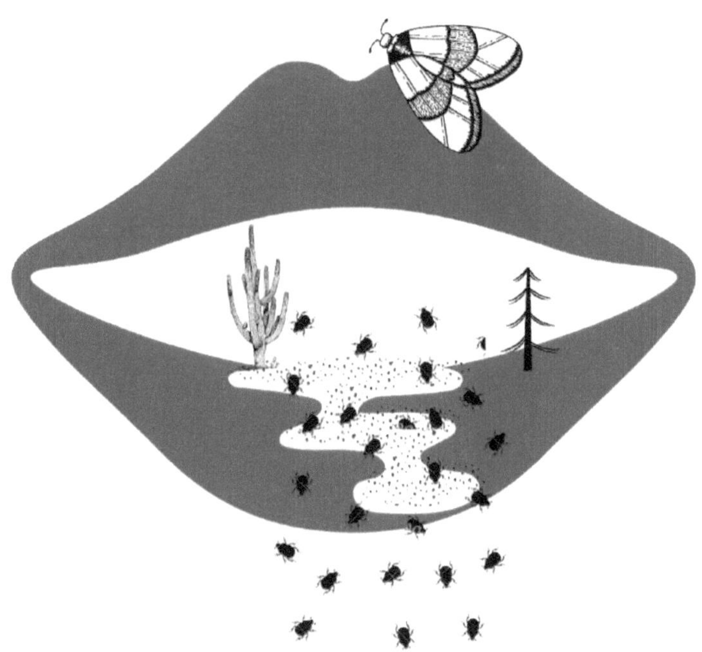

Red Sugar, No More

Just open your mouth and let the lightning come out.
Burn the victim card down to the ground - for you
are so much more than that! You're a witch.
You're a wizard. Open your mouth
and let t h e spiders out!
Unleash your mind;
for sometimes
it's so much
better than
b e i n g
quiet.

<u>Her Victim?</u>

10/11/2018

She glared at me again, today

Her eyes had the fire

      that could burn everything away

Asked me to bow and do as she said

Or else like always she could have me drowned

or it's *off with my head*

Something within lit me up inside

      As I breathed ^{and} closed my eyes

     Opened my mouth and sung a symphony

She wasn't expecting given our history

The bully and the victim no longer existed!

  I ^{talked} back and _{cracked} her grin in _{half}

  As she settled her careful scarf

Shouting at me … going through

 the same statements

like an old draft

              I ^{raised} my voice just as much or more

                 I think I might have just shook

                   that amoral fool to the core

The quiet girl she thought   she could pet like a dog

      Had somehow turned rabid _{because I} bit back

      Loyal or not – no one should push you around

Taking you for granted and telling you about your very own howls

She took it all from me

Red Sugar, No More

My love, my feelings, my positive years

But **"not anymore"** my voice   as sharp as a spear!

How long can one have everything for as per their will?

The world is not robotic so let's not function like that

I don't care if my emotions would take me downhill

I am happy in the pit than living in her *purgatorial heaven*

Out she can go with all her ghastly bits of advice and chill pill

We can all be ***Athena*** – whether you like it or not

So just take that dump in your own shiny pot

Don't you try to throw it on the lot!

Because I can blow you away   l i k e the feathers caught!

Those caged birds with open doors you have chirping for you all day?

The truths I behold can free them all from the spells you foretold

You can't see it – nor can they

But I have the power

to make you all dismay

It's only my heart that keeps

the chaos delayed

So better not break it

Or try to make me sad

Please, don't take my quietness as mere crud

My dear, everyone is a little mad

The school you are studying at?

I graduated from it back in 5th grade

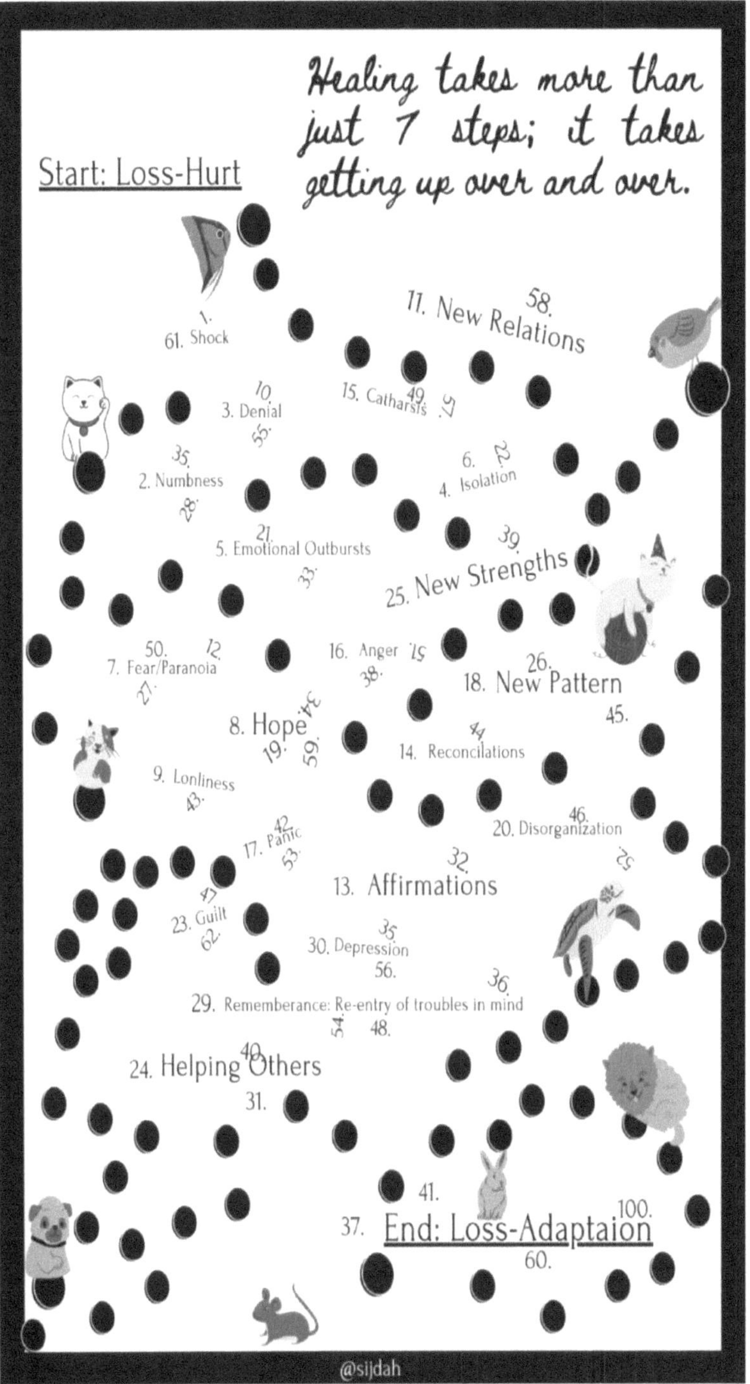
Healing takes more than just 7 steps; it takes getting up over and over.
Start: Loss-Hurt
11. New Relations
58.
61. Shock
1.
10.
3. Denial
15. Catharsis
49.
55.
35.
2. Numbness
6.
4. Isolation
28.
21.
5. Emotional Outbursts
33.
39.
25. New Strengths
50.
12.
7. Fear/Paranoia
16. Anger
26.
18. New Pattern
38.
45.
8. Hope
14. Reconcilations
19.
9. Lonliness
43.
17. Panic
42.
53.
20. Disorganization
46.
32.
13. Affirmations
23. Guilt
47.
62.
35.
30. Depression
56.
36.
29. Rememberance: Re-entry of troubles in mind
54.
48.
24. Helping Others
40.
31.
41.
37. End: Loss-Adaptaion
100.
60.
@sijdah

7:28
Tweet
What's happening?
Who's in this photo?
Lafayatte, LA

"You can count on me ... like 1, 2, 3"

Even when we are old and grey and don't talk – 'cuz I'll be there. Always.

<u>Dear Best Friend(s)?</u>

10/11/2018

I came across your public

social handle 2 weeks ago

Haven't been able to

get you out of my

m   i   n   d

You write well now

I scrolled up and low

I could see how you're

at the edge of your grind

The sombre writing,

the pain –

c

o

m

b

i

n

e

d.

I still love you I know you don't think so

However, I am done trying to be your *gustoso*

I came across that picture where you cropped me

out of the background

I see you two are close now

I opened the caption feeling, expecting,

you might have something for me

I really thought we were the three

The three, ho-ha-ho, musketeers

The powerful triad that

no one could steer

But, oh, that bully I see she's g o o d

                                   Sometimes I wish – I could learn from her

Then, in time, I realize I can easily be her

                         But it's my heart,

                             my

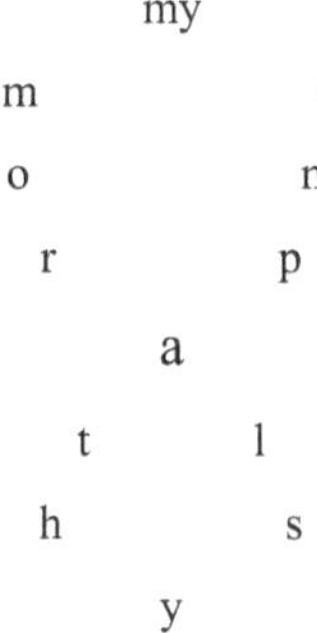

That hold me ₍down₎ and keep me human

I can turn everything around!

                          Ruin everything and make sure they all drown

                               But, oh I am not that, I can't be that

I read the caption it started with "dear best friend"

        I felt a dead butterfly stutter its last dying wing's

                By the time I reached the last word

                    I had a tear and my anger was cold

              I wanted to talk but then I remembered

          You only talked because there was public

        You hugged me when they all could see

        You clicked the photos to show people

                    you are actual ecstasy!

                    I thought I would text you back then too

      Guess what I found when on Facebook I searched you?

               You and the other one still had me blocked.

          Ha Ha, how foolish of me to have expected again?

Red Sugar, No More

I ^{laughed} and _{cried} because people had not lied

When they said – it was only for the public to see!

Just like that at the end of this post
The one of both your surprise birthdays

Joy and west ways!

Just pomp and show

Just meows of crows

There were comments I couldn't see

I knew one was yours & the other Frenchie's

Both of you – still had me cut.

It is sad and good

Both at the ^{same} _{time}

It helped me see the _{down} ^{below}

I had to get stronger and independent

To dig up and grow

It took time to untangle my hair

But today,

you are *just* a bittersweet memory

Both of you I hold close in my heart

but that's all that

I

CAN

do.

I am content   I am at peace

For I wasn't the one --   Who listened to the fleas!

You guys were the ones to not just trade-off our kingdom's keys

But also to lock me down in those dungeons

Sure, call me Hades!

Thank you, my friends   You taught me well

From what to why –   all goes on in my head like a spell

   Not a single human can make my eyes swell

It is all in my head,

   my hands –

     in

       M

       E

    To be and to be

   As I grow like a steel tree.

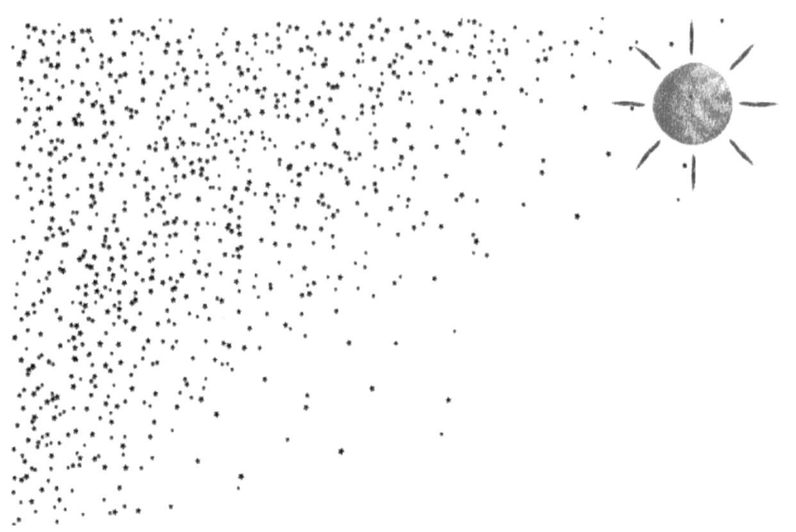

Paranoia (n)

- *A condition where a person always doubts others and themselves.*
- *A condition where all compliments seem too fake to be a reality.*
- *A condition where a person is unable to trust someone even after knowing them for years.*
- *A condition where a person thinks self-sabotage is healthy.*
- *A condition where a person just can't turn off the grinding noises in their brain.*
- *A condition where a person feels that someone is only nice to them because they need something in return.*
- *A condition where a person can no longer differentiate between delusions and reality.*
- *A condition where a person's own mind is their biggest enemy.*
- *A condition where a person is ridden with irrational fears and 'yellow wallpaper' feels.*
- *A condition where a person feels that when people are not talking to them they are either talking **about** them or **against** them. Always.*

<u>Paranoia</u>

10/12/2018

Unpredictability breeds uncertainty

      Just like droplets of blood in a deserted office store

Lipstick smothers on his white checked shirt

      Rain during a strictly sunny day

Poison ivy mixed with herbs

      Same was the case with our fraternity

It was uncertain and unpredictable
We were all too much and too less
for each other -- at the same time
Not a nickel's worth
or that of a dime
We cherished
and smiled

All through the way like a blimey child

      Now, all I feel is numb or aggressive

I don't like seeing anyone to' ^{in similar ways,} suffer

I hate _{those} who tend to be submissive

They remind me of who I used to ^{be}

& how I ended up in the _{gutter}!

      <u>I feel negativity coursing through my veins</u>
      <u>Compelling me to slit and give it an opening</u>

To get it all **out**

      To break it **all**

Be it   me

or

you

or

whoever

I am losing my   self in the process

I wish to go back to how I used to be

The   brightness in my eyes

& optimism in my mind

To make the world

a better place

with

my

h

e

a

r

t

:3

But I fear –

I fear I can never be the same

Because that part of me was somewhat lame

Giving too many chances

Of heartbreaks over and over to the same people

I don't know what to do

Humans have similar tendencies

I

have

too!

We

are

all

selfish ~

Embedded with the idea of heroism

when it comes to us trying to explain ourselves

And pointing the other force as that of a villain

Red Sugar, No More

Was this our purpose?

To make this world a circus

Everyone laughing at each other   without seeing the mirror

Because the reality is *oh just so rare!*

What to do ^{and} what not to do?

Who to trust now _{and} who to waste time on?

Knowing how it ends with humans – every single time!

Why can't I just be enough for myself?

How can I understand the idea of solo-gamy?

Did they grow tired of finding someone to trust?

Or were they too shattered to ever be shattered again --

That they believed it is only their own self with whom they should be lain?

One thought after another

Not one clearly out yet and

not one truly understood

Pondering over everything

like it's my PhD

It's just *oh so crazy*!

How do people find the will to go on?

To be with someone they don't love?

To be in love with someone who doesn't love them?

Or to fall in love with the villain knowing they'd always be that?

Can a good person fall for a bully?

Or is it just a sugar-coated poison going after the other?

How do humans work?

What is the secret behind it all?

How do they not want to stab their hope in the heart

Red Sugar, No More

and just say *"die, bitch!"* ?

Tell me the secret to peace

Give me the calming teas!

My guitar is broken, ^{please}

Someone, _{please}, mend *its* keys

                                       I think I am sadness-internalized

                                           Like it is a piece of my body

I am sadness incarnated ~

I can't live with it …

        but I can't surely live without it too

$$2 \times 2 =$$

$$2 + 2 =$$

$$6 - 2 =$$

$$1 + 3 =$$

$$8 \div 2 =$$

$$16 \div 4 =$$

$$7 - 3 =$$

$$5 - 1 =$$

…………..

Most common answer =

Who told you that everything you think is right? When did you realise that everything you believe is set in stone? Can you choose the correct answer from below? Pick the right feeling – the right answer!

$$|\ 4 + 4 = 8\ |\ 2 \times 4 = 8\ |\ 6 + 2 = 8\ |\ 3 + 5 = 8\ |$$

They are all correct, aren't they? So how can you feel that everything you know is the correct answer to life and, thus, you are validated to play God?

<u>Power</u>

10/13/2018

Power, power.

Is it the <u>highest</u> of towers?

Or a crowd that is <u>all ours</u>?

    How does it help one while downsizing the other?

    Is it a demand of the hour?

      Or just a heart's desire like that of a cake without flour?

            I don't get it why does it matter

            Who eats gold and who doesn't

            Who reaches and who repeats

Because in the end we are all just clouds wandering

around without fighting off the winds

Who designed this intricate

      ladder of

       power?

    Is it like the movement of bowel?

   <u>Free and random</u> – just happens when it does?

              Or is it planned –

           Like <u>the unholy clans</u>?

    Is it knowledge or is it money?

    Cersei **said**; power is power

    But isn't she the one who

     took down innocent

      towers?

Is it good   or   is it bad?

    Who gets to decide about what is what?

   If we are all equal – no caste, no creed

Red Sugar, No More

No colour, no breed

How are some fortunate and some just simply bleed?

Is it greed or is it need?

How about we just hand over the crystal bead –

To whosoever can keep a balance between all

Whether someone is bad,

greedy,

arrogant,

or manipulative

God shall take care of all –

we don't have to be so attentive

We don't know all

We don't know at all

Who's what and what's why!

All we know is the colour of the sky

Let's stop trying for our verdicts to be the law

Because in His court justice will have a tighter claw.

Even if it is something

you can't believe

Karma is real

Mostly because it gives our lives a lot of appeal

Happens or not – just let it be

Stop overthinking and trying to make everyone see

It's not your job nor is it mine

Sweetness always does attract bees

Does that mean the flower should wilt?

Be as you need to –
No one can tell you that you are mere weed!

You are the water, love!
Necessary and desired
Not given much attention to but
the reason for all life to have existed
You can be what you're in –
Adapt and survive,
Or be like the ocean; unapologetic and strong
No one can turn you down or call you wrong
But in the process, just, don't lose yourself
You don't have to be in the list of amoral fools
Or even be their tools

Be free   Be happy
But never at the cost of
making others
feel
c
r
a
p
p
y

*A butterfly doesn't call ahead and choose the perfect day, place or time to go
into metamorphosis – so why do you feel that relationships
could just occur or be done with as per your desire?
Stop putting up lists for ideal 'ships'
– we're all different.*

<u>Expenses</u>

10/19/2018

Let's be friends at <u>our expenses</u>

Going our ways;

Not   our   defences

        making   individualistic

But – my dear, let's not forget …

Expenses have consequences

Lighting each other's world when in need

Is it not the entirety as to why you should

ever pay each other any heed?

Never was it a fair call decided … to be decided

And even if you do have such an understanding --

Just make sure it isn't **one-sided!**

Don't make the other person's heart bleed

While you are high on weed

Don't be a part of that fleet

That names it *friendship* but acts like a cheat

No, you are not the stinky feet

That decides to show up only when forgotten

Why? Because that is just downright rotten

No good for anyone it did

Except for making people build high fences

To keep out similar scrunches

Like I said …

Expenses have their consequences

Please, don't abuse anyone's patience or love

It's like murdering a beautiful white dove
Don't throw away an old pair of gloves
To use the new stoves
It'd end up leaving you crumbled down and above
Don't ruin purity, thereof

Like damaging the correct tenses
You'd end up breaking those
old coffee-scented benches
Where you shared your laughs
Held yourselves up to the humanistic graphs
From all, that's left &
all that's past

No one will come to save your relation
In fact, the world would hold onto popcorns
Pouring more acid to make you trip
And break each other's pretty little hip
Everyone will flip
Putting and dragging each other – bringing upon the end of time!
Because in reality no one is a clown
Everyone would just participate in breaking your crown
No point, thus, of all those frowns
'cuz no one is going to take you to the just court in town

Red Sugar, No More

&

They

will each

time hand

you a

m

a

t

c

h

s

t

i

c

k

Fuel everything up around & beyond

                        To make sure the fire is thick enough

          That your relationship ends up resting

              in the ground below

So, if you want a friendship at your expenses

            Be sure about the consequences

                          Find those who understand

              Not the ones who'd leave for

        just about any bystander

Because *your* good heart or intentions won't C

                  O

                  U

                  N

                  T

For whenever a black sheep is going to bring up

            destructive heartfelt accounts

Your weak-links would turn against you

            No one will care;

           you'd get only stares

Even from those far off affairs, you tried justifying –

Why? Because no one cares if it's a crisis in which you're yourself identifying

If you're not there for them – then it's their time to say *f*ck you*

Don't you understand?

Just understand and accept

Together

never truly

came

with a

forever!

*there is no key to help you out of this.

this thing between you and I
might just be worth a try ~

<u>Haven</u>

11/20/2018

How do I define it?

The thing between you & I

You're the dawn to my dusk

The fragrance to my musk!

Moonlight on the water

Dazzling o'er the sea

Dancing waves all around

Letting one be!

Like rain to the forest

You are valuable to me –

Pushing & pulling

From hell to heaven

Trying not to make anyone

Feel abandoned

Neutrality, equality, equity

But never together –

Out of pity!

In a life full of incidents quite shitty

You're my golden city!

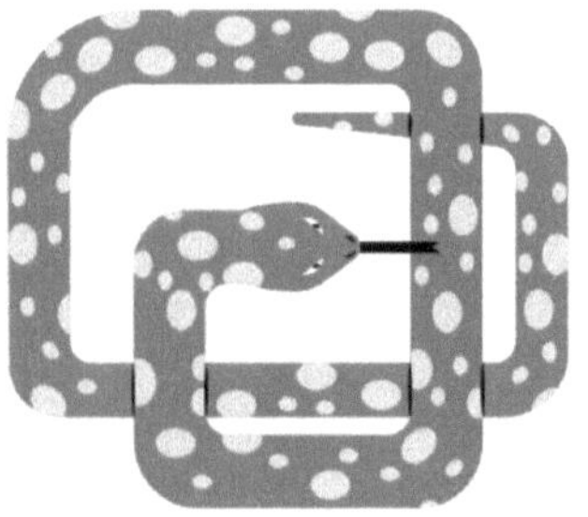

Death does have a certain ring to it – almost makes one romanticize it.

But – should we?

<u>Kill Suicide</u>

11/29/2018

Just open the door and jump out of this car
Let's leave behind all those deep uncleansed scars
Paving the street free, of our burdens
Let's fly above to those magical curtains.

I don't know, dear heart, but even if I do
What do you think the people would assume?
Whether I tried to pull a stunt
Or was it a failure in love?
If my grades were bad
Or all those reputation stats?
Was it the blue or was it the grey
No one would say, just leave her alone now, hey!

If I jump off a tall building, that's an insured way to go
With a one-way ticket that only leads "to" and not "fro"
Would I go to heaven or end up in hell?
But I guess it'd be better than this dirty shell

It's so confusing to just decide
Is it rash or is it wise?
The heart and mind just do not coincide
Would this emptiness go away?
Can that black slug within be banished to nothingness?
Or do I end up all swayed?

If I look into life closely, maybe
I'd find myself an epiphany
It'd touch me within
And turn all the blacks to green … again

Red Sugar, No More

Maybe I should stop turning **and** twisting

Give life another chance but not the negatives

Carry the positives in my arms wherever I go

Help the world be a better place

As little as I may effect

It might just make my life again

something with a purpose –

and also somewhat perfect

Maybe that can kill suicide

And help everyone see the greener side?

* take a chance

maybe there's

more to

life?

Mature (n)

- *A person who does NOT make you feel small.*
- *A person who does NOT tell you how you should think.*
- *A person who does NOT make you feel bad about yourself.*
- *A person who does NOT take advantage of your anxious nature just for the sake of fun.*
- *A person who does NOT identify words, feelings, colours or actions to be gender-biased.*
- *A person who does NOT turn to petty, racist, patriarchal or sexist jokes just to get a few laughs.*
- *A person who does NOT throw tantrums just because they know they are intimidating or loved.*
- *A person who does NOT justify the death of someone from another country, religion, caste, colour, age, creed or breed.*
- *A person who does NOT shame you for having your own experiences.*
- *A person who does NOT share away the words you shared with them in times of trust only to win a few affections.*

<u>Mature</u>

12/21/2018

I am so mature

          And you!?

               Haha, highly unsure

I know my black from white

        Dark from light

          While you dwell in the grey twilight

I know what's right

        Mentally strong

          I just can NOT be wrong!

I am so mature

      While you think you can find the cure?

          -- To sexism, chauvinism and cancer!

Oh, silly child,

    you don't know life

        Can't accept

        Can't be wise

          Be like me!

          Focused and vice

          An unending spice!

I know my reds, my blacks and blues

    You are still stuck between Crimson hues

Red Sugar, No More

Dark is bad, light is white

How can one be just oh-so naïve?

Why can't you think more like me?

With everything defined **predominantly!**

Slim bodies are nice

Fat ones need to pray to *the Lord*

For beauty and love

And everything they'd never get;

Unless their bones I can see!

Else for me, they are a dumpster spree

Why?

Because …

I have all the maturity!

My pains are bigger than your burdens

I can play better badminton

Smash and service – appreciation a gallon!

What do you have other than *sensitivity*?

Grow up, you child!

Stop bossing around

Let me teach you which people to surround!

Come here and sit, with your legs crossed shut

Be quiet and listen to my evil debt

I'll

induce

my mind

within yours

You need to shush

and   accept   all   my   pours!

Put down the names of all those *mature beings* – that shut you up and pour in their ideas – asked or not – they'd always want a piece of our mind. They'll stay here now – not in your head – here.

<u>Dump 'em.</u>

________________   ________________   ________________

________________   ________________   ________________

________________   ________________   ________________

________________   ________________   ________________

Healing
is Messy
but
Necessary!

This

  is the

    beginning

      of an end

        &

          Maybe

           an end

            o f a

             beginning.

Life doesn't stop when we stop nor does it wait for us to start ourselves again.

And that's okay. It'll pass. This'll pass. I'll pass.

Start: Loss-Hurt

1. Shock
2. Numbness
3. Denial
4. Isolation
5. Emotional Outbursts
6. Isolation
7. Fear/Paranoia
8. Hope
9. Loneliness
10. Denial
11. New Relations
12. Fear/Paranoia
13. Affirmations
14. Reconcilations
15. Catharsis
16. Anger
17. Panic
18. New Pattern
19. Hope
20. Disorganization
21. Emotional Outbursts
22. Isolation
23. Guilt
24. Helping Others
25. New Strengths
26. New Pattern
27. Fear/Paranoia
28. Numbness
29. Rememberance: Re-entry of troubles in mind
30. Depression

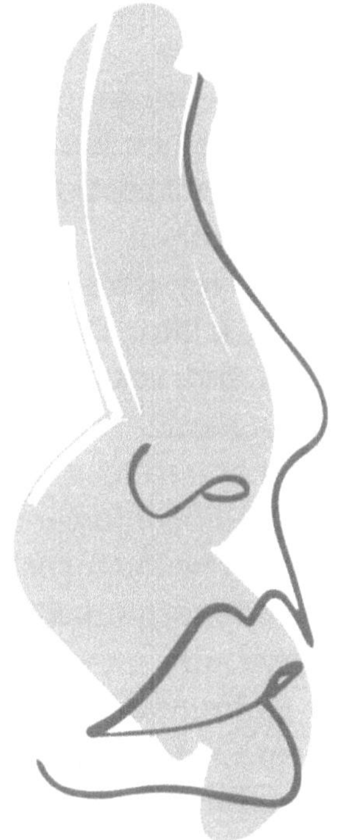

Start: Loss–Hurt

31. Helping Others
32. Affirmations
33. Emotional Outbursts
34. Hope
35. Depression + Numbness
36. Rememberance: Re-entry of troubles in mind
37. **End: Loss-Adaptation**
38. Anger
39. New Strengths
40. Helping Others
41. **End: Loss-Adaption**
42. Panic
43. Loneliness
44. Reconcilations
45. New Patterns
46. Disorganization
47. Guilt
48. Rememberance: Re-entry of troubles in mind
49. Catharsis
50. Fear/Paranoia
51. Anger
52. Disorganization
53. Panic
54. Rememberance: Re-entry of troubles in mind
55. Denial
56. Depression
57. Catharsis
58. New Relations
59. Hope
60. **End: Loss-Adaptaion**
61. Shock

Start: Loss-Hurt

62. Try Again
63. Try Again
64. Try Again
65. Try Again
66. Try Again
67. Try Again
68. Try Again
69. Try Again
70. Try Again
71. Try Again
72. Try Again
73. Try Again
74. Try Again
75. Try Again
76. Try Again

101. Try Again
102. Try Again
103. Try Again
104. Try Again
105. Try Again
106. Try Again
107. Try Again
109. Try Again
110. Try Again
111. Try Again
112. Try Again
113. Try Again
114. Try Again
115. Try Again
116. Try Again

Again
Again
Again
Again
Again
Again
Again
Again
Again
Again
Again
Again
Again
Again

.Try Again
.Try Again
.Try Again
.Try Again
.Try Again
.Try Again
.Try Again
.Try Again
.Try Again
.Try Again
.Try Again
.Try Again
.Try Again
.Try Again
.Try Again

.Try A
.Try A
.Try A
.Try A
.Try A
.Try A
.Try A
.Try A
.Try A
.Try A
.Try A
.Try A
.Try A
.Try A

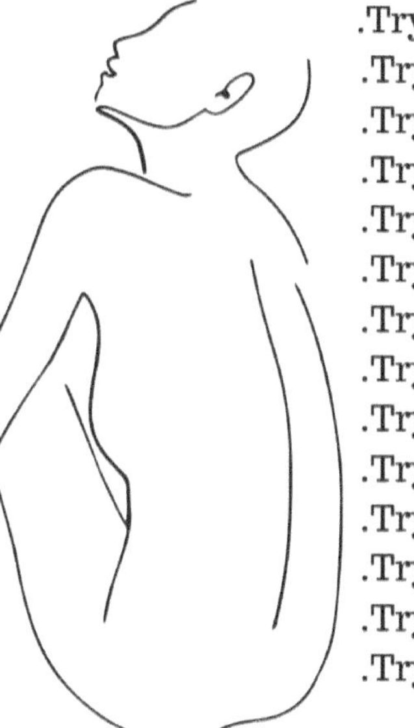

100. End: Loss-Adaptaion

Lets get Personal!

Thank you for taking out your precious time, to join me on this journey from moving out of wallow-town and heading somewhere better and forgiving.

Your emotions, feelings and vulnerability do NOT make you weak – instead, they show how brave you are to be wearing them like a badge! Not everyone has the guts to do so ~

Therefore, be kind to yourself. You are all the stardust collected into one!

Can you see those blueish veins in your wrist filled with haemoglobin?

They are filled with Iron and originally it was only available on a giant red star. In time, our Earth's gravity attracted millions of piece of the supernova to land on it, which in turn brought Iron here. We, in short, are filled with stardust! You are a star twinkling every day to your brightest! A whole 93% of pure star-dust!

You are everything those thousands of starry particles conspired you to be. We are remnants of stars!

www.thesugarseries.com

Special Thanks

For the beta reviews
Habiba, Khoula & Muaaz
Mano for back then
Ashu for all the ideas
Anya for the presence
Rimta for the tough love
Waleedish for all the smiles
Farhana for being the coolant
Nidita for the undying support
Zark for the trustworthy friendship

Fato for the all time entertainment

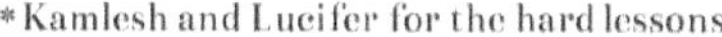

*Kamlesh and Lucifer for the hard lessons

Sneak Peek into
Lime Sugar, Moon Tales

Bro Code

February 2019

In bro code, we believe

Every other gender is welcome to leave!

Law & basic humanistic rules are **not**

 something with what we abide

Only in our brothers, we coincide

The rest can go pull on themselves a homicide ~

M i r r o r,

mirror on the wall

Whose the purest of them all

Not one, not two –

Every girl's got a mental flu!

Taking themselves as harmless mimes

Making each other baseless *shrines*

Born without the *humour* bone

These girls wish to rule our throne?

Lucifer's Birth

August 2019

What is life if not celebrated for and with?

How do we find the will to go on knowing we destroyed so many relationships and mental spaces? It's Lucifer's birthday, AGAIN.

Birthdays have never meant that much to me when it comes to my own but for someone else to feel sad on their day is downright criminal. All my life choices hit me on my day but that doesn't mean I can't make other's born dates better.

It's Lucifer's birthday, after 2 years of working together, it still gives people a boot – people being me – whenever it feels like it. We had our time to leave it all behind and we tried but maybe there was just too much bad blood to let go from both sides. Who knows …

Most of the collaborative family hates it. So I guess I am not the only one who was bitten and hissed at. That makes me feel like a better person. Maybe I am not as toxic as I thought myself to be.

Maybe they left because they wanted to or maybe it all ended because it had to.

Its day will not be celebrated here in the white boxed spaces due to the amoral behavioural patterns with others but maybe we should do something as a peace offering – this year again. No one should end up feeling bad about being unappreciated, at least on their birthdays. No matter how much you want ***Karma*** to hit them.

Printed cards, fresh cake, yellow balloons like its scarf. Maybe we should call in its Frog Prince to join us today as well.

Tsk tsk, there was a time Froggie was a better person … but maybe love changes us all and that's alright.

~~Hello, yeah, bring it in to slither around us so we can celebrate the day our sadness was created.~~

.

.

Oh, hey, so we thought we'd cut a cake for it today and you should totally join us. We work mere block boxes away after all. I'll text you when we are done decorating the black screen room.

.

.

.

.

.

.

.

.

.

.

What's taking it so long?

Other plans, said the Frog Prince.

.

(20 minutes later)

.

.

.

.

.

.

.

.

Happy birthday to you.

Happy birthday to you!

Happy birthday, dear Luci …

Oh, it already left the building because *other plans with my Horcruxes* still exist.

Hey, at least eat the cake!?

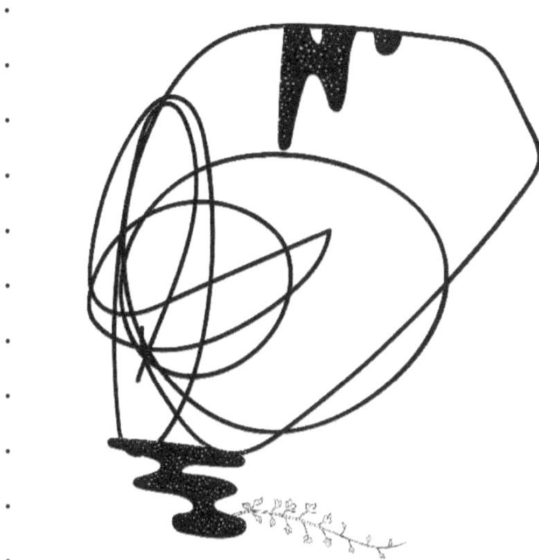

"Um, yeah, I cut it. You all can eat it. It's a bit dry though, great but dry.

Anyways, bye!

Thanks!"

~~You are your own constellation.~~

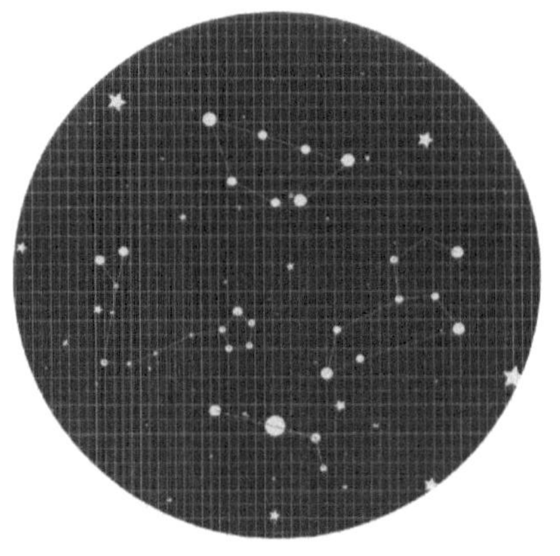

Become your own universe,
You are so much more than a
mere constellation!

Little by little
it's important to keep moving
for the only thing that stays in one
place is dead.

Yes, it's difficult,. Yes, it hurts.
However, it is necessary to keep digging
upwards rather than down.

Pick up that shovel, make your own
tunnel to land. If you won't save
yourself, no one else wiil!
'Bob the builder' didn't wait - he was
the help - you can fix it!

xoxo

Sij.

YOU
NEED
NEED
TO
TO
DIG
DIG
YOURSELF OUT